"My name's Patsy and I wanted a new doll for my birthday, but I got something else instead . . ."

Hana

ERNiE

FERGUS

PATSY

Owen

Francis

MUZZY

Olivia

PATSY, THE PIGLET WITH A NEW BABY BROTHER
A RED FOX BOOK 978 1 862 30578 6

First published in Great Britain by Red Fox,
an imprint of Random House Children's Books
A Random House Group Company

This edition published 2008

1 3 5 7 9 10 8 6 4 2

Text copyright © Red Fox, 2008
Hana's Helpline copyright © 2006 Calon Limited
Hana's Helpline is a registered trademark of Calon.

Red Fox Books are published by Random House Children's Books,
61–63 Uxbridge Road, London W5 5SA

www.**kids**at**randomhouse**.co.uk
www.**rbooks**.co.uk

Addresses for companies within The Random House Group Limited can be found at: www.randomhouse.co.uk/offices.htm

THE RANDOM HOUSE GROUP Limited Reg. No. 954009

A CIP catalogue record for this book is available from the British Library.

Printed in China

Hana's Helpline™

Patsy

THE PIGLET WITH A NEW BABY BROTHER

It was Patsy's birthday and she had lots of presents. But none of the presents was a doll. "Don't worry, Patsy," said her dad. "Your mum and I have a special surprise for you, and it's much better than a doll. It's a lovely new baby brother called Patrick. Do you want to hold him?" Patsy gently held her new baby brother. Maybe he was better than a doll. But then suddenly he was sick, all over Patsy! She quickly put him back in his cot.

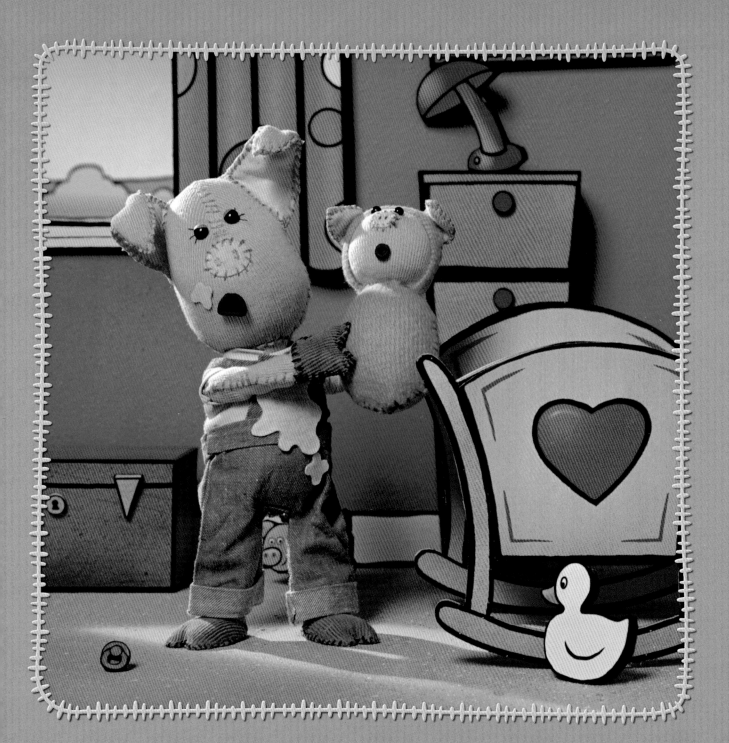

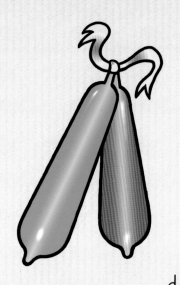

Patsy was very cross. It was her birthday and all she had got was a smelly baby brother. She saw Francis and Fergus going to play with their go-cart.

"Hello, Patsy, did you get the doll you wanted for your birthday?" asked Francis.

"No," said Patsy and stomped off. She decided to ring Hana's Helpline.

When Owen answered the phone, she told him her problem.

"You see, I wanted a doll for my birthday and I got something else instead," she said.

Owen wasn't really listening. "You've got a present you don't want? Then swap it with a friend for something you do want. Bye!"

The next day Patsy decided it was time to take Owen's advice.
"It's very kind of you to take your new baby brother for a
walk, Patsy. I knew you'd grow to love him," said Patsy's mum.
"Yes, Mum," said Patsy. "Bye!" She started to walk down the
street with Patrick.

Patsy decided to go and see Ernie first. He was playing with his toys. "That's a great robot, Ernie," she said. "Do you want to swap it for my baby brother?"

"Do his eyes light up?" asked Ernie.

Patsy shook her head. "No, but he's sick a lot," she said.

Ernie looked worried. "No, I don't want to swap," he said.

Patsy decided to try Olivia next. "Hello, Olivia. Would you like to swap one of your dolls for my baby brother?" she asked.

Olivia looked at Patrick. "He's very cute," she said. "But what's that smell? Has he pooed himself?"

Patsy sniffed. "Yes, I think so," she said.

"Then no thanks!" said Olivia.

"Maybe Muzzy will want to swap," said Patsy. "Hello, Muzzy, do you want to swap your train set for my baby brother?"

"Does he go choo-choo?" said Muzzy.

"Not really, no," said Patsy.

"Then I don't want to swap," said Muzzy.

Francis and Fergus were playing with their go-cart. Fergus was having great fun going down the hill.

"Wheee!" he cried. "This is brilliant."

Back up at the top of the hill Francis suddenly looked worried. "Fergus, look out!" he called. He could see that Fergus was heading for a tree.

Fergus looked up. "Aaaah!" he yelled, but it was too late. He flew through the air and landed in a puddle.

"Fergus!" shouted Francis, then he saw Patsy. "Patsy, help! Fergus is hurt."

"Put him in the pushchair and we'll take him to your mum's," said Patsy.

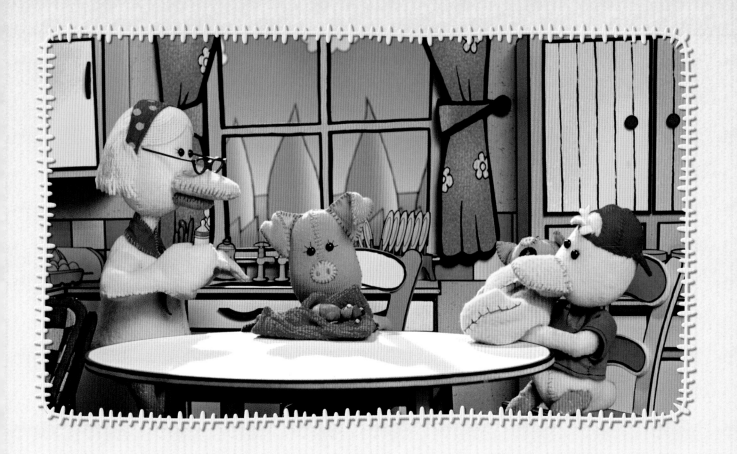

When they got to Hana, she looked carefully at Fergus.
  "No bones broken, but he's very cold," Hana said. "I'll fetch some hot milk. You wrap him in a blanket, Patsy."
  Patsy gently wrapped Fergus and fed him from the bottle.

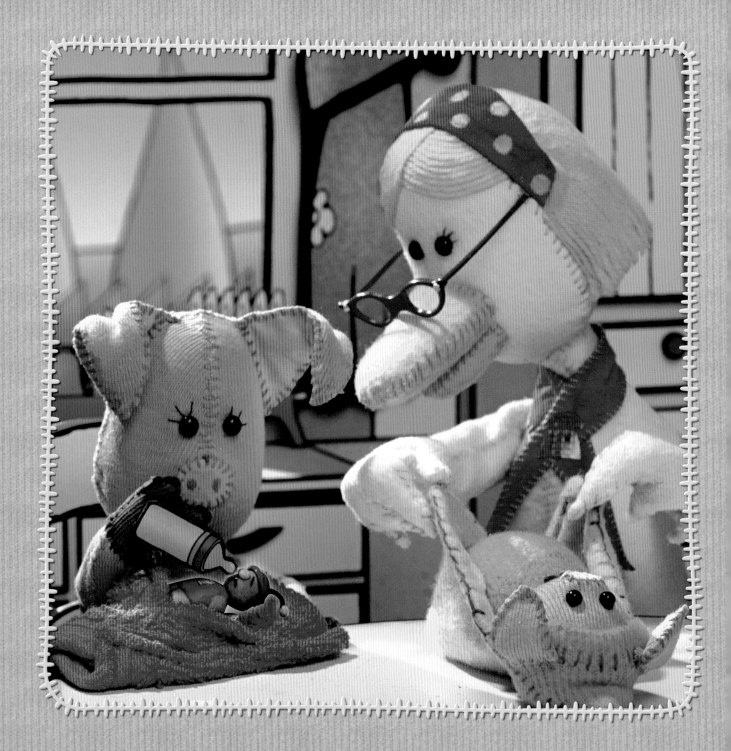

Patrick had begun to cry. Hana went over to him. "Phew! I know what's wrong with you," she said. "You need changing! Is this your new baby brother, Patsy?" she asked.

"Yes," said Patsy. "I wanted a doll for my birthday and when I rang your helpline they said I should swap my brother for a doll!" Hana looked worried. "But no one would swap!" said Patsy.

"Well, I think you're very lucky to have a baby brother," said Hana. "Why don't you ask your mum if you can help look after him? Just like you're looking after Fergus."

Fergus looked much better and he was glowing again.

"Well done, Patsy," said Hana. "He's going to be all right."

The next day when Patsy got home Patrick was crying. "I think he's hungry. Can I feed him, Mum?" asked Patsy. Her mum looked surprised. "Hana says I'm very good at looking after people, especially babies. Babies are much more fun than dolls. You can't feed dolls, can you?"

Patsy's mum handed the bottle to Patsy and she began to feed Patrick. "There you go, Patrick. You're the best birthday present I've ever had."

Hana decided she needed to talk to Owen about his advice to Patsy.

"I didn't know it was a baby she was talking about!" he said. "She just said it was a birthday present and she didn't want it."

"Your problem is that you say things without thinking them through," said Hana. "You should ask more questions before you tell people what to do."

"OK," said Owen. "I'll try that next time, I promise."

Later that day Owen picked up the helpline phone when it rang. "Hana's Helpline. Owen speaking. Yes . . . Yes . . . No . . . Whatever it is, just throw it away!"

Hana's Help Point

Hana's tips if you have a new baby brother or sister

If you have a new brother or sister, don't worry! Hana can help!

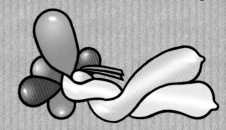

If your mummy is going to have a baby:

★ Ask Mummy to show you where and how the baby is growing

★ Talk gently to the baby in Mummy's tummy. It will be able to hear you and know your voice when it's ready to come out!

★ Ask other children what it is like to have a baby brother or sister

When the baby is born:

★ You can help look after it

★ Give it a present to welcome it into your family

The new baby is very lucky to have you as an older brother or sister. You can:

★ Read it your favourite stories

★ Sing it nursery rhymes

★ Play games – babies like to play peek-a-boo

Big children can:

★ Ride bikes and play with friends

★ Eat food with a knife and fork

★ Read books

★ Be careful with little babies: they are not as tough as you!

BUT REMEMBER: new babies are very small and need lots of looking after

"So remember . . .

. . . if you're in trouble and you need help,
ring me, Hana, on **Moo, Baa,
Double Quack, Double Quack!**"